THIS BOOK IS
FOR the DARLING
CHILD (OR children)
WHO MOST POSITIVELY
ARE ON THE
NICE LIST:

LOVE:

MR. BODDINGTON'S STUDIO

'TWAS THE NIGHT BEFORE CHRISTMAS

POEM BY

CLEMENT CLARKE MOORE

ILLUSTRATED BY

MR. BODDINGTON

FOR PENN + HUCKSLEY.

IT WOULD BE IMPOSSIBLE TO ADORE YOU TWO BOYS MORE . . .

NEVER FORGET TO WATER OUR TREES IN KENT!

—LOVE, M

PENGUIN WORKSHOP
An Imprint of Penguin Random House LLC, New York

The publisher does not have any control over and does not assume any responsibility for author or third-party websites or their content.

Art copyright © 2021 by Mr. Boddington's Studio LLC. All rights reserved. Published by Penguin Workshop, an imprint of Penguin Random House LLC, New York. PENGUIN and PENGUIN WORKSHOP are trademarks of Penguin Books Ltd, and the W colophon is a registered trademark of Penguin Random House LLC. Manufactured in China.

Visit us online at www.penguinrandomhouse.com.

Library of Congress Cataloging-in-Publication Data is available upon request.

ISBN 9780593384077   10 9 8 7 6 5 4 3 2 1 HH

MR. BODDINGTON'S STUDIO

'TWAS THE NIGHT BEFORE CHRISTMAS

POEM BY

CLEMENT CLARKE MOORE

ILLUSTRATED BY

MR. BODDINGTON

'Twas the night before Christmas, when all through the house
Not a creature was stirring, not even a mouse;

The stockings were hung by the chimney with care,
In hopes that St. Nicholas soon would be there;

The children were nestled all snug in their beds,
While visions of sugar-plums danced in their heads;

And mamma in her 'kerchief, and I in my cap,
Had just settled our brains for a long winter's nap,

When out on the lawn there arose such a clatter,
I sprang from my bed to see what was the matter.

Away to the window I flew like a flash,
Tore open the shutters and threw up the sash.

The moon on the breast of the new-fallen snow
Gave a lustre of midday to objects below,

When what to my wondering eyes did appear,
But a miniature sleigh and eight tiny reindeer,

PARIS
N.Y.C.
TOKYO
Shanghai
BERLIN
MOSCOW
DUBAI
Barcelona
MUMBAI
HONG KG
LA
LYON
LONDON
Nairobi
Sydney
Bangkok
Rome
ISTANBUL
RIO
San Fran
SWORDS
DOLLS
COAL

With a little old driver so lively and quick,
I knew in a moment he must be St. Nick.

More rapid than eagles his coursers they came,
And he whistled, and shouted, and called them by name:

"Now, *Dasher*! now, *Dancer*! now *Prancer* and *Vixen*!
On, *Comet*! on, *Cupid*! on, *Donner* and *Blitzen*!

To the top of the porch! to the top of the wall!
Now dash away! dash away! dash away, all!"

As leaves that before the wild hurricane fly,
When they meet with an obstacle, mount to the sky,

So up to the housetop the coursers they flew,
With the sleigh full of toys, and St. Nicholas, too—

And then, in a twinkling, I heard on the roof
The prancing and pawing of each little hoof.

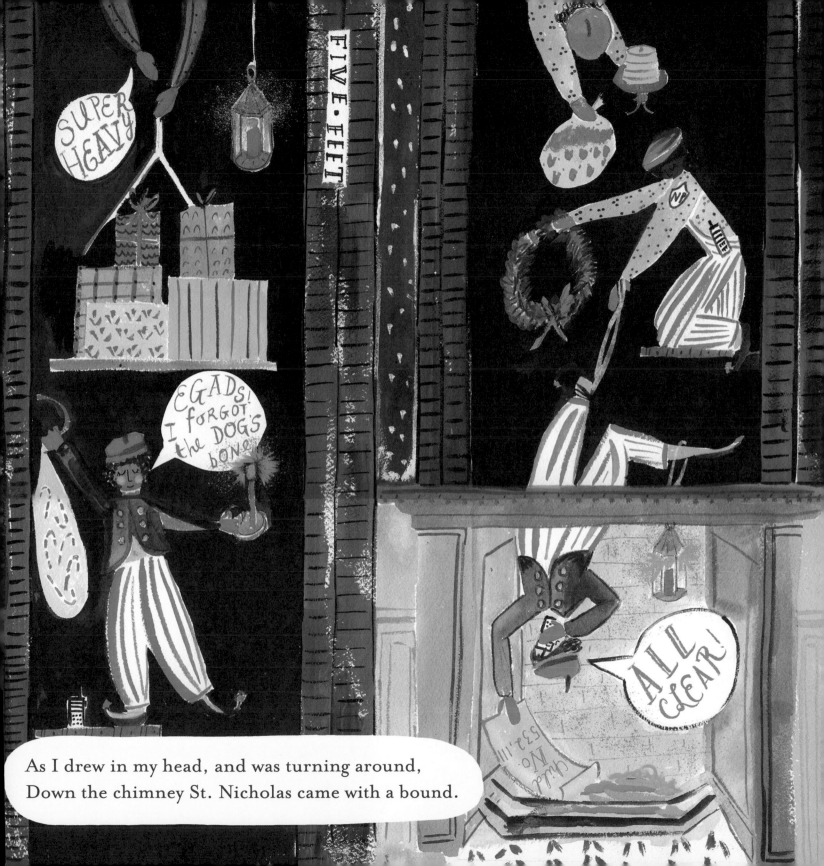

As I drew in my head, and was turning around,
Down the chimney St. Nicholas came with a bound.

He was dressed all in fur, from his head to his foot,
And his clothes were all tarnished with ashes and soot;

A bundle of toys he had flung on his back,
And he looked like a pedler just opening his pack.

His eyes—how they twinkled! his dimples, how merry!
His cheeks were like roses, his nose like a cherry!

His droll little mouth was drawn up like a bow,
And the beard on his chin was as white as the snow;

The stump of a pipe he held tight in his teeth,
And the smoke, it encircled his head like a wreath;

He had a broad face and a little round belly
That shook when he laughed, like a bowl full of jelly.

He was chubby and plump, a right jolly old elf,
And I laughed when I saw him, in spite of myself;

A wink of his eye and a twist of his head
Soon gave me to know I had nothing to dread;

He spoke not a word, but went straight to his work,
And filled all the stockings; then turned with a jerk,

And laying his finger aside of his nose,
And giving a nod, up the chimney he rose.

He sprang to his sleigh, to his team gave a whistle,
And away they all flew like the down of a thistle.

But I heard him exclaim, ere he drove out of sight—
"Happy Christmas to all, and to all a good night!"

HAPPY
CHRISTMAS

OUR HOLIDAY LOG

CHILD	YEAR	BEST GIFT	FAVORITE MEMORY
	20__		
	20__		
	20__		
	20__		
	20__		
	20__		
	20__		
	20__		
	20__		
	20__		
	20__		
	20__		
	20__		